CW0088139s

The Tails of Kit and Kaboodle

Kit and Kaboodle Visit the Rainbow Bridge

Stanley Eugene Horton

Illustrations by Shannon Horton Kendrick

LifeRich Publishing is a registered trademark of The Reader's Digest Association, Inc.

LifeRich Publishing
1663 Liberty Drive
Bloomington, IN 47403
www.liferichpublishing.com
844-686-9607

ISBN: 978-1-4897-3617-8 (sc)
978-1-4897-3616-1 (hc)
978-1-4897-3618-5 (e)

Library of Congress Control Number: 2021910579

LifeRich Publishing rev. date: 05/24/2021

The Tails of Kit and KaBoodle

Kit and Kaboodle
Visit the Rainbow Bridge

I would like to dedicate this book to my Great Grand-Niece, Hannah. Many thanks to Tara Stone and Dave Schroeder for editing and technical help, and to Dennis and Stacy Horton for help in the narrative.

Special thanks to my wonderful sister Shannon for her beautiful illustrations.

Upon a time once, a white cat named Kit lived with her wonderful family on a street in a town beside a beautiful river.

2

Kit was very happy. Her family was a happy, loving bunch of Humanimals. Kit was only sad about one thing: she had been born with only one eye.

On the same street in the town on the beautiful river a black poodle lived next door to Kit the cat. His name was Kaboodle!

Kaboodle was also very happy. He had a wonderful, loving family, but he, too, was sad about just one thing: he only had three legs!

A long, tall fence separated the two families. Kit and Kaboodle couldn't see each other even though they lived only a few feet apart.

Whenever Kit would walk by the fence, Kaboodle would bark loudly, "I know you are over there, cat!"

Kit would hiss at Kaboodle, "I know you are over there too!"

Both Kit and Kaboodle proudly guarded their family but secretly wondered what the other one looked like.

This is what Kit thought Kaboodle
must look like.

And this is what Kaboodle
thought Kit must look like.

Kit's family of Humanimals was white. Kaboodle's family of Humanimals was black.

Sometimes, Kaboodle would ask Kit through a small hole in the fence if she would like to climb over and play.

Kit would always say the same thing: "Dogs and cats are not supposed to play together."

"And besides that"—she didn't know exactly how to say this—"uhm, your Humanimals and mine are different colors too!" Then she added, "That must be why they never talk to each other!"

One night when both Kit and Kaboodle were sleeping in their backyards, a ferocious thunderstorm began.

There was a place along the fence that was covered. Sometimes, during a storm, Kit and Kaboodle would sleep as closely as they could to each other. A storm was coming now, and they were both afraid of thunder and lightning.

After the two finally went to sleep, they had the same dream. Or was it a dream?

When they woke up, they both looked around, amazed at what they saw. They said the same thing at the same time: "Where are we?"

"Why, silly cat and silly dog," came the most beautiful voice they had ever heard, "you are in heaven!"

Kit looked at Kaboodle and shouted, "Kaboodle, I have two eyes!"

"And I have four legs!" exclaimed Kaboodle.

"We really must be in heaven." They ran and played until they noticed lots of Humanimals on the other end of the Rainbow Bridge.

"Dear angel, why are all those Humanimals across the bridge on the other side of the river?" asked Kaboodle.

Hannah the angel replied, "They are all there to meet their pets when it is their time to come to Heaven."

Kit and Kaboodle stared at all the angels but did not see anyone they knew. "It looks like no one is there for us!" cried Kit.

"Oh my," said Angel Hannah with a puzzled look on her beautiful face. "Wait here until I return. I must speak with the wise angel Mabel. She is the Guardian Angel of the Rainbow Bridge."

Angel Hannah returned to Kit and Kaboodle and said, "I am very sorry, but there has been a big mistake!"

Kit and Kaboodle looked on with confused faces.

"It is not your time yet to be in heaven. Angel Briley will take you back to your homes right now." Angel Briley picked up Kit and Kaboodle. "And you must hurry, Kit—there is danger for your family!"

Angel Hannah touched Kit and Kaboodle on their heads and said, "Don't worry, my darlings; we will all meet again at the Rainbow Bridge when it is truly your time."

When Kit and Kaboodle awoke from their strange dream, they were in their backyards. The storm had stopped, but something was terribly wrong! Kit's house was on fire!

Kit yelled at Kaboodle through the fence, "Kaboodle, the wind has blown something into my one eye. I can't see to get into my house to wake up my Humanimals. You must jump over the fence!"

Kaboodle responded, "But I only have three legs; I can't jump that high."

Kaboodle then saw a tree that had been blown over by the storm right where they had fallen asleep!

Kaboodle summoned all his strength and jumped onto the tree and over the fence with a great leap of faith!

Kaboodle raced to the back door of the burning house and barked loudly until Kit's family woke up and escaped.

"Kaboodle, you are my hero!" cried Kit.

Kaboodle stood proudly on all three legs while his Humanimal family came to see what was going on.

"We are very sorry for the loss of your house. Kaboodle, you really are a hero, but it is time to come home now!"

Kaboodle stood next to Kit and refused to move.

Kaboodle's Humanimal father said, "Well, it looks like Kaboodle is not coming without Kit, so why don't you all come and live with us until you have a new home? Tomorrow we will begin to tear down the fences that separate us."

Angels can't be everywhere—
that's why God gave us friends!

And that's the whole
Kit and Kaboodle!

9 781489 736161